Dedicated to all future Bobcat equipment operators.

Early on
Bobcat
the large
in Orang
recruits
the huge
report to

T
cc
h
cc
re
h
th
to
al
w
m
lit

ocat

S185

With help from Mikey, Sergeant Vinny and their coach, the children laid grass and put up lights. Before they could say, "Bobcat Buddies," their new field was finished! The boys and girls had a positively perfect pizza party with their pals, and played soccer late into the night. When Vinny and Mikey returned to Bobcat Bootcamp, everyone cheered, "Mikey, the Mini Track Loader, is ONE TOUGH ANIMAL!"

Early Thursday morning, as a big rainstorm was clearing,
there was still lots of work to be done in Orange City.
The pumpkins at Purdy's Pumpkin Farm were ready to
be harvested, but it was too wet for tractors to do the
job. Farmer Purdy asked Sergeant Vinny for ideas.
Vinny suggested they call on his Bobcat friend, Katie,
the Compact Track Loader, who loved to play in the mud!

They we
and reme
Bobby an
and rumb

Together, Vinny and Katie loaded up every last pumpkin in the pumpkin patch. Then they spread dry hay everywhere, so visitors could enjoy playing with the animals and carving spooky pumpkins. When Vinny and Katie returned to Bobcat Bootcamp, everyone cheered, "Katie, the Compact Track Loader, is ONE TOUGH ANIMAL!"

purdy's pumpkins

On S...
his pr...
befor...
he wa...
effort...

Every last Bobcat passed the final training, and on Sunday morning it was time for the special graduation celebration. All of Orange City's townspeople gathered as the machines rolled down the street to the park carrying supplies for the big celebration. Tony, with the American flag flying high and his strobe light flashing, carried the sparkling award metals.

Fidgety, funny, freckle-faced clowns followed behind Tony, waving eagerly at the crowd. Bobby's bucket was piled high with tasty hotdogs and fresh, sweet oranges. Minny followed with a frosty jug of ice-cold lemonade, a beautiful graduation cake and lots of colorful party balloons that bounced in the breeze!

One by one, the rugged and ready Bobcat recruits rolled up to receive their graduation awards from the Orange City Mayor.

He announced that because they did their best work to serve people, each of them truly was ONE TOUGH ANIMAL. The ceremony was followed by the BIGGEST BOBCAT BASH Orange City had ever seen!